SIMON JAMES

FROG and BEAVER

CANDLEWICK PRESS

First U.S. edition 2018

Library of Congress Catalog Card Number pending
ISBN 978-0-7636-9819-5

18 19 20 21 22 23 CCP 10 9 8 7 6 5 4 3 2 1

Printed in Shenzhen, Guangdong, China

This book was typeset in Goudy Old Style Educational.
The illustrations were done in pen and watercolor.

Candlewick Press
99 Dover Street
Somerville, Massachusetts 02144

visit us at www.candlewick.com

Every morning Frog woke up from under his leaf
and looked out over a beautiful river.

Frog shared the river with his friends: the ducks and their ducklings,
the water voles and their baby water voles.

Everyone lived happily together. It was perfect.

Then one day, a young beaver came swimming down the river.

"Hello, little fella," said the beaver. "I'm Beaver!"

"Hello, friend," said Frog.

"I'm looking for a place to build my first dam," said Beaver.
"It's going to be the biggest and best dam you've ever seen!"
"Well, this is a great place to live," said Frog. "You'll love it here."
"Wonderful!" said Beaver. "I'll get chewing."

But the next day, Frog woke to see that the water in the river was very low.

"What's happened?" asked Vole. "We can hardly swim."

"It's that beaver," said Duck. "Have you seen the size of his dam?"

"Leave it to me," said Frog.
"I'll go and see him."

"Hello, Beaver," said Frog. "Can I have a word?"

"Sorry, Frog. Can't stop to chat. Have you seen my dam? Isn't it fantastic?"

"Well, yes," said Frog. "But it's stopping all the water."

Beaver was too excited to listen.

"This is going to be the best dam for miles around," he said.

"Everyone will love it."

The following day the water in the river was almost gone.

"It's that darn beaver," said Duck. "Who does he think he is?"

"I wish I were bigger," said Vole. "I'd show him a thing or two!"

"Oh, dear," Frog said. "I'll talk to him again."

"Look!" said Beaver, as soon as he saw Frog. "I told you my dam would be the best!"

"But Beaver," said Frog, "why does it have to be so big? We don't have any water left."

"There's lots of water on my side," said Beaver. "Why don't you all move up here?"

"Why do *we* have to move upstream?" Duck groaned.

"I'm sorry," said Frog. "Beaver just wouldn't listen."

"I wish I were bigger," muttered Vole. "I'd teach him a lesson."

When they arrived, Frog introduced everyone to Beaver.

"Hello," said Beaver. "Look at my dam! Isn't it amazing?"

"Humph," muttered Duck.

That evening, Frog helped the
ducks collect sticks to build
a nest for the night.

Then he helped the water
voles dig a new hole.

Finally, Frog fell asleep
under an old leaf.

By morning, Beaver had finished his enormous dam.

"It's brilliant," boasted Beaver. "It's nearly as tall as the mountains!"

"Frog! Frog! Look! It's the best dam in the whole world!"

Frog looked. He saw the huge dam, but he also saw the water about to burst over the top. "Look out, Beaver!" shouted Frog.

Suddenly, branches began
to creak and snap.

Stones tumbled!
Boulders crashed!

And then . . .

whoosh!

The water came crashing through the dam. Beaver was sent tumbling
over and over again as boulders and branches sped by.

And then came the ducks and the ducklings,
the water voles and the baby water voles, and, of course, Frog.
"Swim for the bank!" shouted Frog.

The ducks, the water voles, and Frog all made it safely to the shore.

"Is everybody okay?" asked Frog.

"We're okay," said Vole, "but I think Beaver's in trouble. . . ."

"Is he all right?" asked Duck.

"He's swallowed too much water," said Frog,

"but I know what to do."

Frog jumped up and down
on Beaver's back
until Beaver
began to cough
and splutter.

"W-where am I? What happened?" asked Beaver.

"Your dam burst," said Duck.

"Frog saved your life."

Beaver was quiet for a moment. "How can I ever thank you, Frog?" he gasped.

"Well, we've lost our homes again," Frog said. "Perhaps you could help?"

"Anything!" said Beaver eagerly.

So Beaver helped the ducks build a new nest.
"Not too big, though," said Duck.

And he dug a new hole for the water voles and the baby water voles.

"Not too big, though," said Vole.

And finally, Beaver built a dam for himself — not too big, though.

Everything on the river was perfect again . . .

especially for Beaver's best friend, Frog.